To Our Gaba and to The Village
that brought Angel Birthdays to life.

And Happy Angel Birthday to the Angels who made this all possible:

Grandma GG Lori Assante • Ruth Maria Ingaborg Borgstrom

Aunty Lee Borowski • Joel Ross Driver • Nicole Horoff Eiesland

Helen Fornesi • Diana Lim Garay (Aunt China) • Colonel Stephen L. Garay

William & Louise Garay • Christine Ada Healy (Redmond) • Morgan Jarvis

John & Florence Koment • Sarah Kruckeberg • Sue Anne Lefler

Gramma Kitty Linch • Anna Masetti • Jack Orion Mauldin

GG Kathy McRice • Shannon Carr Nazario • Michal & Auntie Phillis

William F. Redmond • Robert Sills • Bill & Madeline Stenger

The Titas & The Titos • Rich Vliet • Duane Zemaitis

Jean & Walter Zemaitis • Pat & Walt Zemaitis

Copyright © 2013 by Erin Garay. All rights reserved.

Published by Familius LLC, www.familius.com

Familius books are available at special discounts for bulk purchases for sales promotions, family, or corporate use. Special editions, including personalized covers, excerpts of existing books, or books with corporate logos, can be created in large quantities for special needs. For more information, contact Premium Sales at 559-876-2170 or email specialmarkets@familius.com.

Library of Congress Catalog-in-Publication Data

2013935466

pISBN 978-1-938301-94-0   eISBN 978-1-938301-95-7

10 9 8 7 6 5 4 3 2 1

First Edition

Edited by Anji Sandage and Christopher Robbins
Book and jacket design by David Miles
Photographs by Jeannie Sucre
Illustrations for this book were done in watercolor. Illustrations © 2013 by Kristin Abbott

Angel Birthdays

Erin Garay   •   Kristin Abbott, Illustrator

Gracie the Pirate shouts, "You'll never be free!"

This swashbucklin' day begins out at sea.

A holler from Jake, "To the plank, ye shark bait!"

A brother sure makes for a mighty First Mate.

"Ahoy buccaneers! Can you come sit with me?"

An ambush was one thing they didn't foresee.

She held them so tightly, with great loving care.

They knew that their mom had some big news to share.

"God made your Grandma an angel today.

So that makes today her Angel Birthday."

"I feel very sad. I wish she were here,"

Jake says with a sigh. His mom wipes a tear.

"We won't see her again? Is that really true?

That's just not fair. I don't want to believe you."

Gracie stares out the window and up at the clouds,

"So, what happens now?" Gracie wonders aloud.

"Can she see me and hear me and keep me safe too?"

"Yes, she's an angel. She'll help protect you."

Mom gathers them both, a tear in her eye.

"Let's not be sad. She wouldn't want us to cry.

Hugging can help our hearts feel her love."

"You're right! We can feel her love from above!"

"She loved you and praised you and always was there

to listen, to read, or to fix your torn bear.

Now let's make today a day to remember,

A day to cherish a love that's forever."

They crafted their plan. What a fine way
to celebrate Grandma's First Angel Birthday.
"Balloons, cake, and presents are all that we need!
It's bound to be a great party indeed!"

The kids' new balloons
are red, pink, and blue.

Their notes say "Goodbye"
and "I love you," too.

Their bunch of balloons—
"Wow! What a sight!"

It's ready for blastoff.
It's ready for flight.

The countdown begins. Gracie shouts, "One, two, three!"

Jake launches the bunch and they race to be free.

Gazing and grinning, they watch them all rise.

The kids both cheer, "She'll be so surprised!"

An "X" cloud appears and they stand in awe.

"Kids look! There's a kiss from your Angel Grandma!"

They blow kisses back as they all go inside.

Jake whistles and marches. He's bursting with pride.

"Decorations are done. It's time for the cake,"

Gracie declares as Mom starts to bake.

"Her food's what I'll miss. It brought such delight.

She filled up my heart with each single bite.

'Add love,' she would say, 'my secret to baking!'

'Stir, hum, and sing. Food is love in the making.'"

Mom checks her recipe and adds chocolate chips.

She stirs in some love. "It's our sweet Grandma's tip."

The cake is now ready. The candles are lit.

They sing Happy Angel Birthday and oh, what a hit!

"But we still need presents," Jake reminds everyone.

"Good thing your mom is all set to have fun!
These boxes are gifts to be made just by you
to remember your Grandma when you feel blue.
Fill it with memories, your love, and your joy,
a picture of Grandma, a lovable toy."

They sprint though the
house looking for gifts.

Jake finds Grandma's
photo and gives it a kiss.

They find some old cards,
pictures, and lockets,

handkerchiefs Grandma
once kept in her pockets.

"There's just one more thing that I really must find.

It's priceless and special and one-of-a kind!"

"I found it!" Gracie squeals
from the top of her chair.

"Grandma won this for me
at the Old Hometown Fair!"

She places her jewel
inside of the box,

then uses a key to
make sure that it locks.

"What a perfect party! Can we do one next year?"

"We'll host one to keep her fond memory near."

But Gracie looks down and a thought brings a scare.

Could others die too? If so, when? And where?

To answer tough questions straight from the heart,

Mom quickly outlines a "growing up" chart.

She starts out by listing each number to ten.

Then keeps adding rows, again and again.

Ten rows to 100 to show our life's path.

We all will grow older. These kids know their math.

"You are right here on line number one.

It's time for exploring, playing, and fun.

Most become angels at the top of this chart.

That's many adventures away from the start."

Growing Up Chart

91	92	93	94	95	96	97	98	99	100
81	82	83	84	85	86	87	88	89	90
71	72	73	74	75	76	77	78	79	80
61	62	63	64	65	66	67	68	69	70

"We'll smile and play, and we'll make Grandma proud.

We know she'll keep watch from her heavenly cloud."

"We'll try our hardest, do our best every day.

Grandma, we love you . . ."

Angel Birthday Party

Print out our color-in Happy Angel Birthday poster for everyone to color together as a family (available at www.angelbirthdays.com).

Bake an Angel Birthday cake. Choose one of your loved ones' favorite recipes, bake and frost it together. Ask each person in the family to light a candle in honor of your special person.

Buy some Sharpies and eco-friendly, helium-filled, latex balloons. Write loving notes to your loved one, release your balloons, and watch together as your angel receives your message!

Decorate memory boxes with pens, paints, pictures, stickers, etc. Choose an item that holds a special memory of your loved one and place it in the box to share with your family and to create a wonderful keepsake.

Get printables, ideas, and more at www.angelbirthdays.com